By

Amber Belmont

Disclaimer: This is a work of fiction. *Names, characters, businesses, places, events and incidents are either the products of the author's imagination or used in a fictitious manner. Any resemblance to actual persons, living or dead, or actual events is purely coincidental.*

Get early access to my books for FREE! Every two weeks, you'll receive news and updates about my latest paranormal romance novella absolutely FREE.

Sign up now at writing.amberbelmont.com

Contents

Chapter One

I placed the final rose in the table arrangement and stood back to examine my work critically. When you're dealing with a bride who knows exactly what she wants, it was crucial to make sure every petal was in the right place and Jennifer Rafferty had been one of my more demanding customers. Even if she wasn't, it was a matter of personal pride that I never supplied any flowers that were anything less than breath taking and I was particularly pleased with how this combination had worked out.

"That's stunning, Shelby," commented Jess, my assistant, looking over from where she was putting together the bouquets for our delivery driver. "You have such a good eye for design. That wedding's going to be stunning."

"Thanks. Only another thirty to do..."

I grabbed another base and started to recreate what I'd just finished, when I heard the sound of the shop door.

"Could you go get that, Jess?" I asked without looking up, not wanting to lose focus. Once I got my momentum going, I worked fast, but if I was interrupted, I had a tendency to procrastinate before getting back to work and I had a lot I still needed to get done for the wedding.

"Sure."

Jess put down the flowers she was working with and went out to the front deal with the customer while I carried on placing the foliage in exactly the right place. There was something wonderfully meditative about flower arranging. I loved the challenge of creating brand new designs for weddings and went out of my way to give each bride and groom something unique that matched their theme and personalities. This time I was working with peach rosebuds and white, frilly-edged tulips and the effect was spectacular, even if I did say so myself.

If only my parents could see me now. When I'd taken over my aunt's florists, they'd predicted that it would fail within a year.

"Sell it," advised dad when he heard that Aunt Carol had left me the store in her will. "Sell it now while it's still a going concern and you can get a reasonable amount of money. You could get enough to put yourself through college and then go into a more suitable career. You don't know anything about flowers or running a business. If you wait until you've lost all your customers to realize your assets, you'll be lucky if you can find someone who wants to buy the building."

Maybe he was practising some kind of reverse psychology, but there was nothing more guaranteed to make me want to succeed than being told I was going to fail and now the store was unrecognizable from when I'd first taken over. Gone were the dated posters on the walls and the dusty displays, replaced by fresh, off white walls, glorious fresh flowers tastefully arranged to tempt people in to browse and a large window at the front, filling the store with natural light.

The only thing that hadn't changed was the name: Tulips Are Better than One.

Aunt Carol had always said that I had a natural flair with flowers and if the grades I'd gotten at community college had been anything to go by, she was right. Combining floristry with a business studies course, I'd learned everything I needed to transform Tulips from a business that relied on Aunt Carol's handful of loyal customers to get by to a high end floral boutique that regularly made its way into the top ten of local florists. I was aiming to make it into the best national lists before too long.

Not bad for someone who was supposed to have destroyed the business within twelve months.

Jess came in, fanning herself.

"You should see the customer who just walked in," she told me, picking up the order book she'd forgotten to take through with her. "Hot is not the word."

"Really?" I murmured, chuckling to myself. We got a lot of men in the store looking for something to treat the woman in their life. Jess always thought they were good looking, but I wondered what she'd think of them if she knew that they were probably cheating on their wives. Some might say that 26 was too young to be so jaded, but I'd long since learned that men who bought flowers weren't worth the trouble. Sure, there were some who were buying them for a special occasion, but the majority of men who bought flowers were only doing it because of a guilty conscience. That's why I preferred working with brides. At least they gave me hope that true love still existed for a handful of lucky people.

I didn't care how hot this customer was. If he was buying flowers, he wasn't worth the trouble.

"No, I mean it, Shelby. This guy is something else. You can see his muscles rippling through his shirt. He's *ripped*! Whoever he's buying flowers for, she's a lucky gal."

"If you say so." I shook my head, turning back to my table displays as Jess went back out front to finish taking down his order. Although I could have peeked round the corner to see if he really was as buff as Jess said, I needed to focus on what I was doing.

“He didn’t want the bouquet delivered. He’s going to pick them up later.” Jess practically skipped back to her station when she was done. “Maybe he was looking for an excuse to see me again.”

I raised an eyebrow. Jess could be so naïve at times.

“Do you think I could get his number?” she asked, leaning against the counter and resting her head on her hands with a dreamy expression on her face.

“Not if the flowers are for another woman,” I pointed out.

“You’re such a spoilsport,” pouted Jess. “Haven’t you ever heard of love at first sight?”

I sighed and rolled my eyes. “What message does he want on the card?”

Jess peered at her scrawled notes. “All it says is ‘Love C.’” she finally replied. “They could be for anyone.” She squealed. “Which means that he *might* give me his number! Do you mind if I serve him again?"

"Be my guest," I laughed. The enthusiasm of youth! Jess might be a great sales assistant, but she had a lot to learn when it came to men. She'd soon realize that the store wasn't the place to find decent guys.

As the afternoon wore on, I lost myself in wedding flowers. I might be a cynic when it came to love, but I adored working on weddings. I could daydream that I was the blushing bride who would be carrying the bouquet down the aisle and not have to deal with the reality that ever man I'd ever dated had let me down. This was as close as I ever wanted to get to my own wedding.

"Oh shoot!" Jess gasped suddenly, her hand flying to her mouth. "I'm supposed to pick up my kid brother from softball practice. I meant to ask you yesterday if I could leave early, but we were so busy I forgot. Mom's going to kill me if I keep him waiting again." She turned to me, giving me her best puppy dog eyes.

"All right," I sighed. "You can go. I've almost finished the wedding flowers and it's been quiet today."

"Thanks, boss. You're the best! I promise I'll make the time up." Jess practically flew out the store, but was back a moment later looking sheepish. "Sorry, I forgot to tell you. The bouquet with the zinnias over there is the one for Hot Guy. He should be here any minute. If he asks after me, could you give him my number? I really felt like we had a connection, you know?"

"No problem." I waved Jess away. "I'll give him your cell if he asks. Now go get your brother before I change my mind."

"Bye!" Jess rushed off, but when I heard the door go again, I rolled my eyes and walked out to meet her.

"What have you forgotten this time?" I was about to ask, but the words stuck in my throat when I saw who was standing in my store.

"Caleb Love," I breathed, stunned.

"Shelby Roberts. Wow."

Caleb grinned that familiar grin showing off his perfect, white teeth. He'd barely changed since I'd last seen him, his tousled dark brown hair still refusing to be tamed, dark eyes twinkling. Jess was right. He was hot, but I knew all too well that if you got too close, you'd get burned.

"I'd heard that you'd taken over a florist's, but I didn't realize this one was yours. Nice." He looked around the room, nodding his approval.

"Glad you like it," I replied, surreptitiously smoothing my hands down on my apron so he wouldn't notice my palms sweating. *"Stay professional, Shelby,"* I told myself, fighting the urge to yell at him to get out of my store. Screaming arguments were hardly the kind of image I'd cultivated for Tulips, even if the guy did deserve it. "What can I do for you?"

"I ordered some flowers earlier," Caleb told me. "I was told they'd be ready by now?"

I could barely restrain myself from shaking my head. I should have known. He'd run out on another girlfriend and wanted to try and make things up with her. Well more fool her if she fell for it.

"They are," was all I said. "I'll just go and get them for you."

Once I was out back, I shoved my fist into my mouth, biting down hard to suppress the scream that threatened to burst out. Of all the florists in San Francisco, why did he have to walk into mine?

Picking up the bouquet Jess had prepared, I could see my hands were shaking. I regretted letting Jess go early. She'd taken the order. She should be the one to finish it.

"It's all right. You got this." I took a few deep breaths to calm myself before plastering on a fake smile and carrying the flowers out to Caleb.

"There you go." I handed him the bouquet, proud of myself for not hitting him over the head with it. "She's a lucky woman."

"She sure is," nodded Caleb, as arrogant as always. Whoever he dated was *clearly* privileged to have him.

For a moment, he stood there, the smile never leaving his face as the seconds stretched out to what was becoming an unbearably long silence.

"Sorry, Caleb. Was there something else?" I said at last, breaking the tension that had built up.

"That's everything," he replied. "For now. It's good to see you again, Shelby. You haven't changed a bit."

For a moment, I thought he was going to say something else, but instead, he simply turned and walked out of the store, leaving me feeling as though I'd just been punched in the gut. It might have been seven years since I'd last seen him, but the effect he had on me was as powerful as ever.

Chapter Two

"Caleb! Come back!"

My cry woke me up from a nightmare I thought I'd never have again, a nightmare in which I was running after Caleb but he was getting further and further away from me, laughing at my distress.

Pulling myself up to sitting, I untangled myself from my bedsheets, ending up kicking them away in frustration. I hadn't dreamed about my ex-boyfriend for years and now he was back with a vengeance to haunt me.

Great.

I glanced over at the clock by my bed. I didn't have to get up for another hour, but I knew that there was no way I'd be able to get back to sleep after a dream like that, so I got up and padded out to the kitchen to put the coffeemaker on. While it worked its magic, I went to the cupboard where I kept all the things I didn't use anymore but couldn't bear to throw away. Buried deep at the back was a box I hadn't opened since I'd left home. Pulling it out, I sifted through old report cards, certificates and books until I unearthed something I hadn't seen in years.

Pouring myself a cup of strong, black coffee, I curled up on the sofa, my high school yearbook in my lap. Taking a deep breath, I turned the pages until I found what I was looking for.

There, staring up at me, was a photo of me and Caleb on our prom night, taken just after we'd been crowned king and queen. I was smiling at the camera, but Caleb was looking down at me, adoration on his face. He really hadn't changed much over the past few years. If anything, he'd gotten even better looking as he'd matured and my fingers traced his jawline in the picture, remembering the feel of his skin against mine, the taste of his lips when we kissed.

Anyone looking at this picture would have thought we were destined to stay together. We were the epitome of high school sweethearts who were deeply in love, the ones who were going to marry and fill a house full of babies. In fact, if you read through all the comments my friends had written in my book, most of them talked about the pair of us staying together forever and what a cute couple we made.

The night that picture was taken, Caleb and I made love for the first time on a blanket up in the woods overlooking the school grounds. Although neither of us had any experience, it wasn't anything like I'd expected. My girlfriends who'd slept with their boyfriends talked about how quick and awkward it was and warned me that it wouldn't be anything special, but it was with Caleb, it really was. He was so tender and gentle, taking his time to make sure that I was ready for him and by the time he entered me, I was lost in bliss. Coincidentally, just as he finished, fireworks went off to celebrate prom, making us laugh at the timing.

"I promise to always make you see fireworks," he told me, kissing me deeply. Young innocent fool that I was, I believed him. Yet only a couple of short months later, he disappeared without warning, not even bothering to write and explain why he'd abandoned me.

It had taken me years to come to terms with how he'd left, going over and over in my mind all the possibilities, questioning what I'd done to deserve being dumped like that. I'd never have thought that Caleb could be so cruel. I'd never imagine there was that side to him, not the sweet, kind boy I'd fallen in love with.

I'd had no warning that anything was wrong. In fact, the day before he left, we were talking about our plans to go traveling around Europe. Even after spending so long trying to figure out what he was thinking, I still didn't get how he could have sat with me, surfing the net to decide where we should go first when he must have known that he was about to walk out. It took a special kind of mean to keep up the pretence until the last minute.

I'll never forget the day I found out he was gone as long as I live. I rang his cell when I woke up, just as I always did, to say good morning. We used to love chatting while we lay in bed, thinking about what it would be like when we were finally able to get a place of our own and have our early morning conversations lying next to each other. This time, there was no reply.

It wasn't like Caleb not to answer, but I figured that maybe he was in the shower or something, so I sent him a quick text asking him to call before heading down to get some breakfast.

When I hadn't heard anything by mid-morning, I knew that something was up, but I still wasn't too worried as I headed over to his house. His parents' car was missing from the drive, so I figured he might have gone out on an errand but I knocked on the door anyway, just in case he was home, and was stunned when a stranger answered the door.

"I-is Caleb there?" I eventually stammered.

"He's gone," came the curt reply.

I frowned and shook my head slightly in confusion. "Gone where?"

The man shrugged. "I don't know. All I know's Curtis rang last night and asked if I could watch over the place for a while. Said there was some kind of family crisis."

"Family crisis?" Panicked butterflies started flapping about in my stomach as I imagined Caleb lying in a hospital bed somewhere. "What kind of crisis?"

"Couldn't say. Unless you're family, 'course."

"I'm Caleb's girlfriend," I told him anxiously.

"So not family then." The man started to shut the door, but I put out a hand to stop him.

"Wait! Caleb and I were going to have a future together. He wouldn't have just left without telling me where he was going. Didn't he leave a message for me or something?"

The man sighed and tutted. "Look, miss. You seem like a really sweet gal and I wish I could help you more, but I can't. I don't know where they went and even if

I did, I wouldn't be able to tell you without checking with Curtis first and I'm not likely to speak to him for a while."

"Well when you do, could you at least ask Mr Love to get Caleb to call?" I pleaded.

"I'm sorry. I can ask, but if I were you, I wouldn't get my hopes up. In fact, if I were you, I'd forget all about him. I don't think they're going to come back any time soon."

He shut the door and this time I didn't do anything to stop him. As I turned to leave, tears started rolling down my cheeks and by the time I was by my car, I was sobbing, huge wracking sobs that felt as though they were going to tear my body apart. I slid down to the ground, resting against the car door as I turned my head to the sky and wailed.

I didn't understand what had happened then and I still don't understand now. The difference is that now I don't care. I spent years going over every tiny detail of our relationship, desperately trying to come up with an explanation for what happened and in the end, the only thing I could think of was that Caleb simply wasn't the man I though he was. He'd shown me that all the beautiful promises in the world don't mean a thing.

It took years to piece together my broken heart, but when I finally felt ready to start dating again, I'd never met anyone who made me see fireworks and I didn't see the point in being with someone who didn't make me feel special. I'd been single for a while now and I'd never been happier. I could focus on my business without the distraction of a man and business was blooming in every sense of the word.

Trust Caleb to choose this moment to walk back into my life. All I could do was hope that he'd choose another florist next time he needed to say sorry. Still, whoever he was buying flowers for was welcome to him. Maybe he'd grown up and had learned how to treat her with respect. I wasn't going to hold my breath though.

The sound of my alarm filtering through from my bedroom told me that I'd spent longer walking down Memory Lane than I realized and I shoved the yearbook back in its box before going off to get ready for work. It had nothing to do with Caleb's reappearance that I spent a little longer over my appearance than usual. No, nothing at all.

I looked at myself in the mirror. A simple white vest clung to my curves over a pair of light gray slacks. I was never going to be what you'd call skinny, but I liked my figure the way it was.

I'd once gone a date with a guy who'd told me I'd be so pretty if I 'just lost a few pounds.' Unsurprisingly, I didn't invite him back home for coffee, despite his heavy hints that he'd be willing to do me the favour of lowering his usual standards. I wasn't going to starve myself for the sake of a man who didn't appreciate me and I certainly wasn't going to sleep with him.

On a whim, I decided to put on a little more makeup than normal, a dash of green eyeshadow to complement my hazel eyes and a bit of lip gloss, blowing a kiss at my reflection. Take that, Caleb

Love! This is what you lost when you walked out.

The extra time I spent over my appearance meant that I was late leaving, despite having woken up early. Luckily, when I got to the store, I found Jess already there, bustling about preparing the orders for the first morning delivery.

“Thanks so much for letting me leave early yesterday,” she gushed. “I got to my brother just as they were finishing practice. If I’d left it any later, mom would have killed me for leaving him with the coach again.”

“No problem,” I replied. “Just next time give me a bit more notice, okay? Yesterday was quiet, but I can’t guarantee that I can let you go just like that next time.”

“I know, I know. I’m sorry. I should be more organized.” Jess picked up the list of deliveries that needed to be prepared. “That’s why I came in early to make it up to you. I’ve already done most of the orders for this morning. There's just a couple more bouquets left."

I took the list from her and scanned it. "All right. You do the $30 standard and I'll take the super deluxe."

As I gathered together the flowers I needed, I wondered not for the first time whether it would be worth hiring another sales assistant who could help with the admin. So far, I'd managed to get everything done with just Jess helping, but the way things were going, it wouldn't be long before I wouldn't be able to cope if she wasn't around and I couldn't expect her to put in the kind of hours I did.

I made a mental note to put a sign up in the window later. That's how I'd found Jess, so maybe I'd get lucky a second time.

"So did Mr Hottie ask about me when he picked up his flowers yesterday?" asked Jess.

"Mr Hottie?" I frowned, pretending that I didn't know exactly who she was talking about. "Oh, you mean Caleb?"

"Caleb?" Jess did a double take. "Do you know him?"

"Unfortunately, yes," I replied. "And if you know what's good for you, you'll stay away from him."

"Seriously?" gasped Jess. "But he seemed so nice. Are you sure you're talking about the same guy?"

I glared at her, daring her to disagree with me.

"Shame," sighed Jess. "I could get lost in his eyes for days. I can't believe that anyone as good would be that bad."

"Looks can be deceiving," I said through gritted teeth, as I accidentally crushed one of the blooms I was putting into the bouquet. "Dammit! Now look what you made me do. Honestly, Jess, if you were a little more focused on your work and a little less worried about how attractive our customers are, you'd get a lot more done about the place."

"Sorry," muttered Jess, rolling her eyes when she thought I couldn't see. I almost called her out on it, but stopped myself. For all that she could be a little flaky, Jess was a good assistant and the customers loved her. It would be ironic if she walked out right when I was thinking about getting a third pair of hands to help because we were so busy.

“Look, why don’t you go out front and work on the displays?” I suggested, trying to defuse the frosty atmosphere between us. “I’ll finish up the deliveries.”

“All right.” Jess slouched off to the store while I turned my attention to flower arranging. As always, I found myself getting lost in the moment as I worked on creating perfect bouquets. We sold a range of standard arrangements as well as custom designs, and I loved the freedom that came when someone left me to decide what would work. Right now, I was putting together flowers of varying shades of blue, offsetting them with the occasional pink. I was so engrossed in what I was doing that I didn’t hear the customer coming into the shop, not that it mattered. That was up to Jess to deal with.

“Shelby?”

I jumped at the sound of my assistant's voice. "Don't creep up on me like that," I scolded, dropping the stem I was holding. "You almost made me destroy another flower."

"Sorry. It's just that there's someone out there who wants to see you."

"Can't you deal with it?"

Jess shook her head, her face red with excitement. "He's really insistent that he has to speak to you."

"He?" My heart sank as I hoped that it wasn't who I thought it was.

"Mm-hmm." Jess nodded, beckoning excitedly for me to follow her.

Taking a deep breath to calm myself, I couldn't help but feel glad that I'd taken the time to do my makeup properly this morning. Let Caleb see what he'd been missing out on all these years.

"Go out back and finish the orders," I told Jess when I saw Caleb standing in the middle of the store. I saw her peering round from the back and I raised my eyebrows, gesturing with my head for her to get lost. She quickly pulled her head away but I knew that she'd be listening in, so I was going to have to watch what I said. I didn't want to give her any more fuel for gossip.

"What can I do for you, sir?" I asked.

"Sir?" Caleb laughed. "Seriously?"

"I'm very serious." I folded my arms. "Now what do you want? Don't tell me." I gazed around the store. "More flowers. You must have really messed up. Again."

Caleb held up his hands in surrender. "I don't blame you for being mad at me."

"Mad?" I scoffed. "You flatter yourself. I don't feel anything about you."

One corner of Caleb's mouth lifted. "You almost manage to say it like you mean it. You forget. I know you too well. You never could lie to me."

"Unlike you," I pointed out bitterly.

"I never lied to you," Caleb protested. "I just-" He cut himself short. "Look. I didn't come here to fight with you. I actually wanted to ask you if you'd come out to dinner with me."

I couldn't hold back the laugh that erupted. "Dinner? With you? You must be nuts. I sold you flowers yesterday because I'm a professional, but that's as far as it goes."

"Please, Shelby. Let me explain-"

"No." I held up a finger to cut him off. I couldn't bear to hear him opening up old wounds. "The time for explanations has long since gone. I waited for months, years even, for you to get in touch and you never did, so I moved on. Now all of a sudden, just when my life's really good, you waltz in here and expect me to fall at your feet like a dumb schoolgirl. Well you can forget it. I'm not the silly girl I used to be. You can't charm me any more."

"If you would only listen to me for five minutes..." Caleb ran his hand through his hair, a clear sign that he was getting frustrated. He wasn't the only one who remembered the other's tells.

"You need to leave my store, Caleb. Now." I stalked over and opened the store door for him, gesturing for him to go.

"Fine." Caleb came after me, stopping to stand so close that for a second I thought he was going to lean forward and kiss me. "But don't think I'm going to give up on you. Not now that I've found you again."

I closed the door behind him, leaning back against it as I closed my eyes, fighting back tears. My hands were shaking as I reached up to tuck an imaginary stray hair behind my ear, pulling myself together so I could get back to work.

I didn't know what Caleb had wanted to tell me and I didn't care.

Yeah, right, Shelby. You keep telling yourself that and maybe you'll believe it someday.

Chapter Three

Not long after Caleb left, I took not just one, but two large orders, both for new clients, which meant that I wanted to go above and beyond to make sure that they became repeat business. Those orders combined with a seemingly never ending stream of customers walking in meant that by the time Jess turned the sign on the door to 'closed', there was still a lot that needed to be done before I could go home for the day.

"Could you stay an extra hour?" I asked Jess hopefully. "Just to help me get the buttonholes done. I'll pay you double."

"Sorry, Shelby." Jess shook her head, shrugging her shoulders. "I'd love to help, but we've got family visiting and I promised mom I'd help her cook. Any other time and I'd totally be there."

"Don't worry about it," I said, trying not to let her see how annoyed I was at the thought of being there until midnight. "You go home and have fun."

“Yeah, right,” drawled Jess. “Mom and Uncle Bill bicker all the time over things that happened when they were kids while Grammy complains about the food, even when it’s done exactly the way she likes it. It’s a whole bundle of fun!”

“Ah well. At least they’ll be gone soon,” I laughed. “It’s not as though they live with you.”

“It can’t be soon enough,” muttered Jess, grabbing her bag and heading out to the door. “See you in the morning!”

I was wrong when I thought I’d be in the store until midnight. It was gone one by the time I was ready to lock up and it wasn’t the first time I’d had to put in long hours by myself.

“That’s it.” Even though I wanted nothing more than to go home and curl up under my duvet, I fired up the store computer and quickly put together a ‘Help Wanted’ sign. I printed it out and fixed it to the window before I headed hope, exhausted. Hopefully I’d find another Jess before the week was out.

#

"Nice sign," commented Jess as she walked in the next morning. "You're not looking to replace me, are you? Because I can tell mom that she needs to get another babysitter."

"No, no," I replied. "Nothing like that. The opposite, in fact. I figured that it was about time we got some more help about the place. Until we do, you and I are going to be rushed off our feet – we've got another wedding booked and I've had a few new enquiries I need to put together some samples for, so if your mom *could* get another babysitter that would be great."

"Where do you want me to start?" Jess rolled up her sleeves and came to stand next to me as I talked her through the order book and the work I wanted her to do. However, I didn't even get half way through the list before Jess clapped a hand over her mouth.

"I am so sorry," she gasped as she pushed past me and back to the employee's restroom. The sounds that came from the cubicle didn't sound good at all.

"Jess?" I knocked on the door. "Are you okay?"

"Not really," came the miserable reply. "I think it's something I ate. I guess Grammy had a point after all."

"I'll be out front if you need anything," I told her, going back to start prepping the bouquets for delivery, but by the time she emerged, one look at her pale face told me that the only thing she needed was to go home.

"Go on. Get out of here," I ordered.

"No, no. I'm fine," Jess protested, but she was swaying as she tried to arrange some flowers and a moment later, she was back out in the restroom.

When she finally appeared, I was waiting for her, her things in hand.

"You need to be in bed," I said, shoving her bag at her. "You're in no fit state to deal with anything right now. Get some shut eye and feel better."

"But what about all the orders? You can't do it all alone," Jess argued, desperately trying to hold it together.

"You let me worry about that," I said firmly, as I gently pushed her towards the door. "One look at you and you'll scare my customers away."

"All right. But I'll be back tomorrow, I promise," Jess insisted as she left. I wasn't so sure. Whatever she had, it looked serious.

I headed back and put together that morning's orders as quickly as possible, barely managing to tie the final ribbon before Jed, my delivery driver, arrived. As he headed off, the phone rang, just as a customer walked in to browse. After I'd completed the phone order, I barely had enough time to ring up her sale before the phone went again.

It was as if the universe knew that I was on my own and was sending all this extra business my way out of spite. I needed a miracle if I was going to get through the day.

I heard the door go just as I was on the phone to one of my brides, calling to make sure that everything was fine.

“Just a moment.” I held up a finger, turning on my brightest smile to reassure the walk-in that I'd be with them as soon as possible. My smile faded when I saw who it was.

Caleb.

I just about managed to keep my irritation out of my voice, as I finished up the call as quickly as possible so that I could get rid of him.

“I'm not in the mood for your games,” I warned him. “It's just me today and I've got a lot to get through, so why don't you turn around and head on back to wherever you came from.”

“I saw your sign in the window,” he replied. “I figured you could use an extra pair of hands.”

“I can,” I confirmed. “But not yours. So if you could-”

I was cut off from finishing my sentence as the phone went again. I waved Caleb away, a pained expression on my face as I pulled out the order pad. Annoyingly, he stayed right where he was, so I put my hand over the receiver.

“Leave!” I hissed, but Caleb just grinned. That man wasn’t going to know what hit him once I’d finished with this call.

As I scribbled down the details of the order, the door went again and a customer walked in. I turned to tell them I’d be there in a second, but Caleb got there first.

“How can I help you today, ma’am?” he beamed.

I was too professional to roll my eyes as the woman simpered, easy prey to Caleb’s natural charm. I watched her flirting with him as he took her round the shop, making suggestions until he’d put together a rather expensive selection.

I hung up the phone, just as Caleb brought her flowers to the wrapping area. “Can I leave this with you to finish up, Shelby?” he asked as if he were the one in charge.

I narrowed my eyes. “Of course,” I replied through gritted teeth, as he moved away to tidy up the displays.

I waited patiently for the customer to drag her gaze away from Caleb’s behind. I could understand why she’d want to feast her eyes. There was no denying that his body was amazing. He could have any woman he wanted. All he had to do was snap his fingers and they’d come running. I always thought how lucky I was that I was the one he’d chosen, that I was the one who got to ruffle his hair, run my hand down his chest. Just thinking about it was enough to make me blush.

“What’s the occasion?” I asked the woman, as much to force myself to stop staring at my ex-boyfriend as to finish up the sale.

“What?” She finally turned to look at me, but I could tell that she was still fantasizing about Caleb. “Oh. Yes, it’s my mom’s birthday.”

“I’m sure she’ll be thrilled when she sees these then,” I smiled, as I got out the birthday cards for her to choose from, while I wrapped the flowers so they'd stay fresh.

"Your sales assistant is a real asset. You should give him a raise," she advised, handing over her credit card when she was all done.

"Caleb? Oh no. He doesn't-"

"Need one," he finished smoothly, coming over when he heard his name. "Being able to work with Shelby is payment enough. Now you remember to come back and let me know what your mom thought of the flowers. We have a loyalty scheme for our regular customers and there's nothing like the smile on your mom's face when she gets a surprise bouquet."

"I'll definitely be coming back," gushed the customer as Caleb escorted her to the door. I watched as she handed him her business card, clearly hoping he'd call.

"There you go." Caleb tossed the card onto the counter. "Add her details to your mailing list. Unless you'd like me to do it for you?"

"Nice try, Caleb." I folded my arms. "You don't work here, though."

"Really? Because I could have sworn I just sold that woman some flowers. I talked her into doubling her spend as well. She only wanted carnations, but I persuaded her to be a little more adventurous."

"Yes, well, you always were far too charming for your own good. But much as I appreciate your efforts, I need someone in the store who's a little more... reliable. I can't have staff who are going to do a disappearing act when they feel like it."

A shadow flickered across Caleb's eyes, his smile fading a little.

"You can trust me, Shelby. I'm not going to let you down."

"No, you're not," I nodded. "Because I'm not going to give you the chance. I don't know why you're refusing to take a hint, so let me spell it out nice and clearly for you. I'm. Not. Interested."

Caleb opened his mouth to reply, but we were interrupted by the door.

"How can I help?" asked Caleb, striding forward to meet the customer so that it was impossible for me to interfere without making myself look bad. I had no choice but to let him serve them, especially since another one walked into the store right behind them.

If I thought business had been brisk already, that was nothing compared to the rest of the day. It pained me to admit it, but Caleb was incredible with the customers. When he turned on that brilliant smile of his, women were putty in his hands and I watched as he made customer after customer part with more of their hard earned dollars than they'd planned.

By the time I was ready to close the store, I knew that I wasn't going to have to look at the books to see how well we'd done. Single handed, Caleb had managed to double my sales in just one day.

“Same time tomorrow, boss?” he asked, leaning over the counter as I added up the takings.

“I’m not your boss, Caleb,” I sighed, losing count of the coins in my hand.

“Come on, Shelby. After a day like today can you really turn me away? That was the ultimate in job interviews and I passed with flying colors.”

“You were good with the customers, sure,” I conceded.

“And we got on well, didn’t we?”

I felt my stomach twist as I thought back over the day. We’d been so busy I hadn’t had a chance to stay mad at him and it had been just like old times, the pair of us laughing and joking together. Caleb seemed to be able to read my mind, knowing exactly what I needed him to do with little training and being able to let him handle the customers made it easy for me to deal with all the other, more complicated tasks. It was true that it had been one of the best days I'd had in a long time and it was all down to him.

"You're a dangerous man, Mr Love," I whispered at last, turning back to the till. I fought to keep my focus on getting the figures right and not drop any coins because my hands were shaking so much.

"Shelby..."

Caleb put his hand over mine, forcing me to stop what I was doing. I closed my eyes, inhaling his scent. I hated that he still had such a powerful physical effect on me. Every part of my body was crying out for him to touch me. If he tried to kiss me, I didn't think I'd be able to tell him no.

He turned me to face him, gently running the back of his hand down my cheek. I wanted him so, so bad, but I couldn't risk him hurting me again. I didn't think I'd survive him walking out a second time.

"Please, Shelby," he said gently. "Let me take you out to dinner tonight. I want to explain why I left the way I did."

I shook my head, not trusting my voice.

"All right, a drink, then," he urged. "Just one little drink. Come on. You saw what a good team we make. All I want to do is talk. Can you really send me away without hearing what happened?"

The minute he said the words, I knew he was right. I'd managed to fool myself into thinking I didn't care why he'd abandoned me, but the truth was that if I didn't take this chance to find out why he'd skipped town, I'd spend the rest of my life wondering. I'd had enough sleepless nights already because of him.

"Okay," I finally agreed. "You can take me out tonight. But you need to let me finish up here and I want to go home and change before we go anywhere."

"Great!" Caleb just about managed to restrain himself from punching the air. "I'll pick you up from your place at eight."

"No." I shook my head. I wasn't ready for him to know where I lived and I didn't want to leave myself without a way of getting home if we had an argument. "I'll meet you."

"All right," said Caleb. "There's a bar on Chestnut Street – the Tipsy Pig. Do you know it?"

"Sure," I nodded.

"I'll meet you there at eight."

"I'll be there," I told him. "Just make sure that you are."

"Trust me. I wouldn't miss it for the world."

"I wish I could," I whispered as he left. After the day we'd had together, I wanted to trust him. I wanted to welcome him back into my world and pick up where we'd left off, but there was nothing he could say that would convince me it was worth the risk.

I'd meet him to night and hear him out. Maybe the answers he gave me would give me closure. But once he'd had his say, then that was it. I was going to find someone else to help me round the store and it would be goodbye Caleb.

Only this time, it would be *my* decision.

Chapter Four

Clothes lay strewn around my room as I tried to decide what to wear. What outfit do you wear to send out the right signal to your ex-boyfriend who you may or may not still be in love with? I wanted to look drop dead gorgeous with a 'yeah, I'm hot, but you can't have me,' vibe. I didn't want to give Caleb any ideas. Things were complicated enough without having to deal with Caleb making a pass at me, but at the same time, he needed to know what he'd been missing out on all these years.

In the end, I settled on a simple black dress with a halter neck that hinted at cleavage, while the waistline clung to my hips, flaring out to emphasise my curves. I kept my makeup light, adding just enough to heighten my features but without making it look as though I'd gone to any real effort.

Tying my hair up, I let a few tendrils curl artfully down to frame my face and I finished the look with my grandmother's moonstone pendant.

“Not bad, Shelby,” I commented to my reflection. “Not bad at all.”

I’d spent enough time getting ready. I couldn’t put it off any longer. It was time to go and meet Caleb and find out what was so important that he’d had to vanish into thin air.

I managed to find a parking spot on the street not too far from the Tipsy Pig and took a few deep, calming breaths before I got out of my car. Now that I was actually here, I wasn’t so sure that I wanted to talk to Caleb after all. How was I to know that what he told me would be the truth? It would serve him right after walking out on me that I did the same to him. Let him learn what it felt like to be abandoned.

Only it wouldn’t be the same. Caleb knew where I worked. If I bailed, I didn’t doubt that he’d just show up tomorrow and the next day and the day after that until I finally agreed to let him tell me whatever it was that was so important he vanished without a trace. When Caleb wanted something, he didn’t stop until he got it. I might as well get this talk over and done with and then he could go and crawl back to wherever it was he'd been hiding all these years.

I smoothed out an imaginary wrinkle from my skirt, straightened my dress straps and pushed open the door to the bar, scanning the room for Caleb. The place was packed and it took a while for me to spot him by the bar. I squeezed through the crowds and tapped him on the shoulder.

"Shelby! You made it," he beamed, making to come and give me a hug before thinking better of it, so that we ended up shaking hands awkwardly.

"I thought you wanted to talk?" I asked.

"What?"

I stood on tiptoe so I could speak into his ear. "I said, I thought you wanted to talk? This place isn't exactly quiet. What are we doing here?"

"Ah yes." Caleb put his unfinished drink on the bar. "Follow me."

He beckoned to me to go after him. I frowned in confusion when he led me straight out of the bar and onto the street.

"What kind of game are you playing, Caleb Love?" I demanded, hands on hips. "First you invite me out for a drink so we can talk, then you take me to a bar that's so loud I can barely hear myself think and *then* you make me leave before I can order anything! I'm not in the mood for games, so you better give me one good reason why I shouldn't just turn around and go straight home."

"I'm sorry, Shelby. I really want to tell you everything, but it's difficult."

"Oh you poor thing," I sneered, turning to leave.

"It's not like that." Caleb put out a hand to stop me.

"Let go of me or I'll rip your arm off," I snarled.

"Look, it's just… I…" Caleb ran his hand through his hair in frustration. "It's easier to show you what happened than try and explain, all right?"

“Show me?” I frowned in confusion.

“I promise you, it will all become clear real soon. I asked you to meet me here because it was close to the Bridge. If it’s all right with you, I want to drive you somewhere and then you’ll understand everything. Please, Shelby. Come with me and let me show you why I did what I did.”

Every instinct in me screamed to get out of there. What could Caleb possibly have to show me that would make sense out of any of this?

But there was a vulnerability in his eyes that made me want to give him a chance, so somehow, I found myself nodding. “All right. But if I find that you’ve been wasting my time, then so help me...”

“I’m not wasting your time, I promise,” Caleb assured me, relief all over his face as he led me to where his car was parked.

“Oh no, you don’t,” I said as he opened the passenger door for me. “I’ll follow you. My car’s just over there.”

"Please, just let me drive you," begged Caleb. "Where we're going, there are a few tricky turns and trails. It'll be so much easier if you let me take you. I promise I'll bring you back as soon as you ask me to."

I don't know what it was that made me agree. Maybe it was the long day at work, maybe he was wearing me down. But somehow, I found myself throwing caution to the wind and climbing into the passenger seat as Caleb buckled himself in next to me.

"If you think that I can afford to pay you the kind of money that will get you a vehicle like this, you're sadly mistaken," I warned him as I ran my hand over the leather trim of his new Chrysler.

"Yeah." Caleb had the good grace to blush. "Is it wrong that I came in to help you out because I wanted to be near you rather than because I needed the money?"

"It kind of is," I replied, although I couldn't help but be flattered. "I mean, I really do need someone else in the store, someone who's going to stick around permanently. What am I supposed to do when you decide that you're bored and want to move on again?"

"Bored?" Caleb turned to look me in the eye. "Is that what you think happened?"

"I guess," I shrugged. I wasn't going to tell him that I also thought that he'd decided I wasn't pretty enough or good enough for his family and a million and one other things, none of them good.

"Jeez," he breathed. "I know I can't apologize enough for what I did to you, but if I'd known that's what you thought, I would have come back sooner."

"What did you think I thought?"

"I thought you found someone else, that you got over me almost as soon as I'd gone."

"Are you kidding?" My eyes could have popped out on stalks. I couldn't believe what I was hearing. "What on earth gave you that idea?"

“I heard that you were dating Brandon James.”

“Brandon?” I frowned. “I never dated Brandon. Who told you that?”

Caleb’s skin turned even redder. I used to find his tendency to blush endearing and now I was grateful that he couldn’t hide his embarrassment from me.

“Nobody had to tell me. I saw you.”

“Saw us? What are you talking about?”

“I came back for you.”

“You came back?” My heart leaped into my mouth. “You couldn’t have. Somebody would have told me you were in town. I don’t believe you.”

“Believe it or not, it’s the truth,” Caleb shrugged. “I went to your house. You have no idea how hard it was to knock on the door, knowing how much I must have hurt you, but I did it. When your dad answered, I didn’t know what to expect. He’s the kindest man I know, but for a moment, I thought he was going to punch me. Instead, he told me that you’d gone out with Brandon and warned me to stay away if I knew what was good for me. I couldn't leave without knowing the truth, so I went to find you. When I saw you sitting in our booth at the diner, I knew your dad was right and I should leave you to get on with your life, so I left and didn't look back."

He turned the key in the ignition and pulled out, using his driving as an excuse to avoid my gaze.

"But I never dated Brandon, I swear," I protested. "I used to tutor him in math. Sure, he made a pass at me once, but I made it very clear that I wasn't interested and he'd regret it if he tried again. He was a perfect gentleman after that."

"So your dad lied to me," said Caleb grimly.

"It wasn't like that. He didn't actually tell you I was dating, did he?" I pointed out.

"Well, no," conceded Caleb.

"He must have been trying to protect me. You weren't there."

"But I came back and he didn't tell you, did he?" Caleb asked.

"No, he didn't, but you didn't see how upset I was. He was the one who wiped away my tears, encouraged me to go out and get on with my life when I wanted to curl up and die. I guess he just didn't want me to get hurt again."

"Did it work?"

Caleb glanced at me. I bit my lip, unsure of what to say. I didn't want to feed Caleb's ego by telling him about all those sleepless nights when I stayed up crying or the nightmares that had started up again. I couldn't blame dad for wanting to spare me all that pain again, even as I wished he were still alive for me to ask him what he'd been thinking.

"Where exactly are we going?" I asked, glad for the chance to change the subject when I realized that we were heading in the direction of the Golden Gate Bridge.

"It's a secret," came the mysterious reply. "All I can say is that it's somewhere that's been in my family for generations and only the chosen are allowed to visit."

"Only the chosen?" I laughed. "What is this? Some weird cult?"

"No, nothing like that." Caleb laughed with me. "You haven't got anything to worry about. You're perfectly safe with me."

The way he made me feel, I wasn't sure that I could agree with him. I didn't think that I would ever be safe with Caleb. Not at all.

Chapter Five

"Are we going to Muir Woods?" I asked when I recognized the direction we were going.

"Not exactly. I told you we were going to a family place, remember?" replied Caleb. "And we're almost there."

He indicated to take a small turn off on the right that was so narrow, you could easily miss it. There was no sign post and the road was only big enough for one vehicle with no passing points, so I hoped that we didn't meet anyone coming in the opposite direction. I could understand why he hadn't wanted me to drive down here. I wasn't exactly the most confident of drivers and this kind of trail was my worst nightmare.

After about ten minutes of driving in silence as I let Caleb focus on where he was going, the road opened out into a clearing with space for about twenty cars to park. We were the only ones there as he pulled up into a space, but it was clear from the tracks that there were times when it was packed.

"What is this place?" I asked as Caleb switched off the engine.

"I told you. It belongs to my family. Or, more accurately, to my clan."

"Your clan?" I had no idea what he was talking about. "What do you mean?"

"Come with me and I'll explain," he promised for what seemed like the thousandth time. "We're almost there and then you'll understand everything."

He held out a hand to me and I took it without thinking, as he led me down a dirt track and deep into the redwoods.

"Watch your step," he cautioned as the track narrowed and we pushed through the undergrowth. It might be that the family gathered here a lot, but it didn't look as though anyone came to this section of the land very often.

"Almost there..." Caleb let go of my hand to hold a branch out of my way, beckoning for me to go on ahead. I pushed through and gasped when I saw what was waiting for me.

The moonlight filtered through the trees, the nearly full moon nearly as bright as the sun, revealing a stunning woodland glade. Ahead of us, a small pool was fed from a little waterfall, the moonlight glistening off the water so that it looked almost as though it was liquid silver trickling down. There was magic here. It felt as though any minute a fairy would come floating out from the trees to swim in the water.

“This is incredible,” I gasped. “I had no idea your family had anything like this.”

“It’s a closely kept, family secret,” Caleb told me. “I wasn’t told about it until I was brought here. Only a select few are allowed in.”

“A select few including ex-girlfriends?” I hated to ruin the mood, but I was no nearer to an explanation and if Caleb thought that bringing me to some private forest was going to change anything, he was going to have to think again. It might be the most romantic place I’d ever been, but that didn't change the way he'd run out on me.

"Not ex-girlfriends, no." Caleb shook his head, as he moved into the middle of the clearing, starting to unbutton his shirt.

"Woah there, cowboy." I backed away, holding up my hands to shield my eyes. "When you said you had something to show me, I didn't think you were talking about your body. You promised me explanations and if you think you can distract me with your muscles, you can think again. You can put them away right now."

I peeked between my fingers to see if his torso was as ripped as I remembered. It wasn't. It was even more toned. The guy had been working out! For all my protests, it was *very* distracting watching him undress.

"Relax, Shelby," Caleb soothed. "I'm only taking off my shirt because I don't want to ruin it. You're safe from me."

Part of me didn't want to be safe, but I continued to try and avert my eyes until

Caleb was down to his tighty whities. I couldn't help but sneak a glance at the bulge in his briefs. I bit my lip as my body remembered our times together.

"Look at me, Shelby," Caleb said softly.

I dropped my hand, abandoning the pretence that I wasn't enjoying the sight of his nearly naked body.

"All right, so you've been to the gym a few times since I last saw you." I feigned indifference. "Am I supposed to see your abs and be so overcome with lust, I forget about how you treated me?"

"That's not what I came here to show you," Caleb replied. "This is."

He closed his eyes, clenching his hands into fists. A strange mist rose up, swirling around him.

"Caleb? What's going on? Are you okay, Caleb?"

When the mist cleared, there was no sign of the man I'd come here with. In his place was a bear. A large, grizzly bear.

I gasped as I realized that this was his secret. Caleb was a shifter!

Chapter Six

I stood there, rooted to the spot in shock. Of all the things Caleb could have been hiding from me, this was the last thing I expected.

The bear roared, beckoning with its head to come closer. At first, I couldn't move, but when he roared again, somehow managing to make it reassuring, I forced myself to take one step, then another until I was standing next to him.

Hand shaking, I reached out to feel his fur. To my surprise, it felt a lot like stroking a really, really large dog. His fur was a little courser and longer, but if I closed my eyes, I could imagine that I was next to a large Newfoundland instead of a grizzly bear powerful enough to rip me to shreds.

As I ran my fingers through his fur, I gradually became more and more relaxed, my initial fear gradually subsiding. This was Caleb. This was who he really was.

Caleb made a strange noise, jerking his head towards his back.

“You want me to climb on?” I asked, hardly daring to believe that this was really happening.

Caleb nodded, kneeling down to make it easy to climb onto him. Grabbing two large handfuls of fur, I pulled myself up, throwing my leg over his back. I leaned forward and rubbed my face against his fur, loving the way the lingering scent of his aftershave mixed with the bear smell. I inhaled deeply, drinking him up with every inch of my body.

When he was sure I was sitting comfortably, Caleb roared and reared up, forcing me to cling tightly to his back as he took off, running through the forest. I’d ridden horses when I was younger, but it was nothing like this. As Caleb pounded through the trees, I became used to gripping with my knees, adjusting to how broad he was beneath me, eventually becoming bold enough to sit up, reveling in the feel of the wind rushing past me.

"Woo-hoo!" I whooped, the sound echoing through the trees as Caleb roared in answer.

I don't know how long we spent running. It could have been minutes or it could have been hours. Either way, I didn't care. I was with Caleb and it had never felt more right.

At last, Caleb trotted up to a log cabin tucked away in the middle of the forest. As I slipped off his back, the mist rose up around him, dissipating to reveal his human form again. His very naked human form.

"I'll just go and fetch some clothes," he called over his shoulder as he padded inside, completely at ease in his skin. "Make yourself comfortable in the lounge and I'll be with you in a minute."

I followed him into the cabin, enjoying the view of his toned buttocks as he walked. It seemed a shame to let him cover up, but we still had a lot of talking to do and I wasn't going to be able to listen to a word he said while I was confronted by the sight of his body.

There was no denying that he was still the most attractive man I'd ever met.

The front door led into a large, open area with sofas and chairs spread about, I guessed for clan meetings. I took a seat at a sofa close to a big, unlit fireplace, waiting for Caleb to return and fill in the details of what had happened all those years ago.

"Drink?"

Caleb stalked into the room, wearing jeans and a tight, white shirt that left little to the imagination. As if I needed to be reminded of how rock hard his stomach was.

"Definitely."

Caleb went over to a globe and tipped up the top to reveal a drinks cabinet. "Whiskey?"

"Whatever's easy." The truth was that although I didn't usually like hard liquor, right now, I didn't care what I drank. I just needed something, anything, to steady my nerves.

Caleb crossed over and handed me a tumbler, which I drained in one hit.

"Gah!" I spluttered as the alcohol hit my throat. "I'd forgotten how much that burned."

"I do have wine, you know," Caleb smiled, holding up a bottle of red. "But I figured you could do with something a little stronger."

"Thanks. You were right. In fact, I'll take another one, thanks." I held up my glass for Caleb to refill, the alcohol quickly working its magic to relax me, its warmth spreading through my body. I rested my head against the back of the sofa, sighing as I finally allowed myself to unwind.

"Why didn't you just tell me about this when we started dating?" I asked as he handed me my drink. "Heck, Caleb. You know me. It's not as though I was going to judge you for being a shifter."

"I know," sighed Caleb. "And I would have done. But I didn't know myself. When I said that this place was a closely guarded family secret, it wasn't the only thing we keep on a need to know basis. Shifting runs in my family but it's been known to skip a generation or two. My dad isn't a bear and he and mom were hoping that I would follow in his footsteps. I know that times have changed and we're no longer hunted for our fur, but there's still plenty of prejudice out there. They just wanted to keep me safe. They figured that they could worry about what to do if I shifted if that day ever came.

"I was completely in the dark about the family history until I started showing the signs. A new shifter can be unpredictable, but because dad hadn't been through the change, he didn't know how quickly it could hit. When he noticed that my eyes had changed color one night, he didn't want to take any chances. A newly shifted bear is unpredictable and they didn't want to risk me accidentally hurting someone, so they took me out here to the clan base to see if I really was a shifter or if it was just some minor fluke. They only just made it in time. My claws started growing as we drove and I accidentally ripped up the seats on the journey. It's one of the reasons why we have this land. It's a haven where new shifters can learn how to control their powers safely under the guidance and protection of the clan."

"So that was the family emergency?" I asked.

"Yep," Caleb nodded. "You have no idea how hard it was, discovering that I was a shifter and suddenly having to learn how to control my powers when nobody had ever even mentioned that it might be a possibility. My world was turned upside down overnight and not only did I have to adjust to being a shifter, I had to do it knowing how badly you must be hurting. It killed me not being able to talk to you. You have no idea how hard it was to be away from you when we'd never gone a day without seeing each other in all the time we'd dated. If they'd just told me that shifting ran in the family, I could have warned you about it, let you know that I might have to go away one day so you could decide if you wanted to wait for me or walk away."

"I'd never have walked away from you," I said, putting my hand over his as I'd done so many times before. Caleb turned his hand over so that his palm was against mine, rubbing his thumb up and down against the sensitive skin of my wrist. That simple touch sent a shiver running through my body and I had to force myself to pull my hand away. I wasn't ready to get take that next step yet, not until we'd said everything that needed to be said.

"I know," sighed Caleb. "And if I'd just been able to write to you, then I know you would have been there to meet me when I was finally ready to leave the clan base. But you have no idea how exhausting it is to shift between human and bear form when you're not used to it. I don't have much memory of those early days as a shifter. They passed in a haze of sleep and bear rage. My clan were there to make sure I didn't hurt anyone, myself included, which meant that for the first few weeks I was here, I spent most of my time in bear form, learning how to control my beast so that I'd never be a threat to anyone. Even though I could still think as a human, it's impossible to hold a pen in a paw so I could get a note to you. Believe me, I tried."

He grinned, but it was tinged with sadness for all the time we'd lost.

"Once I'd tamed my beast," he went on, "the next step was to master the change. I spent hours focusing on different parts of my body, learning how to shift from one form to the other."

He held up a hand, mist swirling round it to reveal a single bear paw while the rest of him remained human. "I can control every part of my body you know."

"Every part?" I raised an eyebrow.

"Every part," he leered, a twinkle in his eye. Now it was my turn to blush.

"Anyway," he continued, "I lost track of how long I was here. By the time the clan decided that I was ready to return to the world outside, I was stunned to discover how many months had passed. I knew that it was too much to hope that you'd have waited for me, but I couldn't leave without seeing if you still love me, so I went over to your house…"

"…which is when my dad told you that I was with Brandon," I finished.

Caleb shrugged. "I didn't want to believe him, but when I saw the two of you together, I had to accept it. I figured that if you'd moved on, then it would be better to let you go and not open old wounds by forcing you to choose between us. I loved you enough to want you to be happy, even if that happiness wasn't with me. So instead, I moved away, took a job with my uncle, traveled the world. I never forgot you, though. It didn't matter how far away I went, you were always on my mind and recently I've been having dreams about you. That's what made me come back to find you. Among shifters, dreams are taken seriously. They can be omens if you know how to read them."

"Omens?" I asked sharply, recalling my nightmare of a few days ago.

"Yes," nodded Caleb. "In my dream, someone's taking you away from me and I'm running after you, calling your name, but you get further and further away. In despair I shift into bear form and finally manage to rescue you." He narrowed his eyes, peering closely at me. "You have the same dream, don't you?"

"No, well, yes, well, not exactly," I stammered. "It's very similar. Someone's taking you away and I'm trying to catch up, but I'm too slow. There's nothing I can do to stop you leaving. All I can do is watch you go."

I didn't want to cry in front of him, but as the first tear trickled down my cheek, it was followed by another and another until it all came flooding out.

"It's okay," soothed Caleb, gathering me up into his arms and stroking my hair. "I'm here now and I'm not going anywhere."

"That's what you said before, though," I sobbed. "How do you know that the dream doesn't mean that something's going to take you away again? We've only just found each other. I don't think I could cope if I lost you a second time. People split up for a reason. Perhaps it's better if we keep things as a beautiful memory and leave our relationship where it belongs – in the past."

"You don't mean that," Caleb shook his head, holding me tight.

"I do," I insisted. "You broke my heart and it's only just healed. I'm not strong enough to go through that again."

"You won't have to," Caleb promised. "Because I know what the dream means."

"Really?"

"Yes. I had to hear from you to be certain, but now that I know you're having the dream too, there's no doubt. You're my mate. We're destined to be together forever."

He leaned forward and started to kiss the tears away from my face. A low moan escaped me as he began to gently lick the edge of my lips, raining soft, tender kisses around my mouth. He knew exactly where I liked to be touched and I felt a tightening between my legs as he lightly stroked the sensitive line that ran from behind my ear and down my neck.

I couldn't help it. I kissed him back, running my hands through his hair. It still felt more like fur and I grabbed a handful of it, loving the feel of it against my skin.

Caleb took hold of my waist and rolled me round so that I was sitting on his lap. I could feel the hard bulge in his pants and I gently swayed, rubbing against him, making him grow even harder.

"Careful, Shelby," he growled. "I want to take my time with you."

I giggled. "Don't worry," I replied. "We've got all night."

I sat up and reached behind my neck to untie my dress straps, letting my top fall down. With one deft movement, Caleb undid the clasp at the back of my bra, revealing my breasts.

"You're beautiful," he breathed, as he gently fondled my breasts. He leaned forward to take one of my nipples in his mouth, rolling his tongue over it to make me gasp, clenching fistfuls of his hair in my hand to keep him there.

"Your turn," I smiled at last, when Caleb came up for air. I reached down and pulled his shirt over his head, running my hands down his chest to rediscover the feel of his muscles.

"What do you think?" he said. "Do you prefer hairy or smooth?"

I laughed as he made hair grow on his chest and just as quickly made it disappear again. "Let's see you repeat that trick with the rest of your body," I decided, getting off his lap so that I could pull down his pants. At last, he was naked, as I kneeled between his legs to admire his firm, erect cock.

Taking it in my hand, I began to massage it up and down, as Caleb closed his eyes and threw his head back. "So you can change the size whenever you want?" I asked.

Caleb nodded. “Whenever *you* want.”

As I watched, his cock widened to the point that my hand could barely fit around it.

“I can mold myself to your body,” he told me. “I can be exactly what you want me to be. Your wish is my command.”

“Is that right?” I arched an eyebrow and leaned forward to run my tongue over the head of his cock, making him gasp.

“Oh yes,” he moaned, as I took his cock into my mouth, enjoying the taste of him. All that time learning how to control his body had clearly paid off. Stamina was not the word.

“All right,” he said at last. “You need to stop that. This night was supposed to be about you and you’re not even naked yet.”

“We can soon fix that,” I grinned wickedly, standing up to let my dress pool to the floor, leaving me in nothing but my panties. I turned my back to him, looking over my shoulder as I shook my butt at him, hooking my fingers into the side of my underwear to slowly slide them down my legs. Turning, I swung them round, letting them fly off into the air, not caring where they landed.

"Come here, woman!" Caleb lunged forward, scooping me off the floor and lying me down on the sofa. Putting his hands on my thighs, he spread them wide, leaning forward to flick his tongue against my pussy. I couldn't remember the last time I'd been so wet. Caleb and I had gotten to know every inch of each other's bodies when we were dating, but that was nothing like this. He'd always been a sensitive lover, but now he really knew how to drive a woman wild.

"I need you, Caleb," I cried. "I need you now!"

"Whatever you say." He moved up until he was lying over me, supporting himself on his arms so he could look me straight in the eye. I could feel his cock rubbing against me, teasing me, taunting me.

"Please, Caleb, do it. Do it now!"

At last, he finally entered me, moving slowly at first before plunging deep as we found our rhythm together. I wrapped my legs around his butt, pulling him towards me as I could feel myself building to a climax.

Just as he always promised he would, Caleb made me see fireworks.

“Was that all right?” he asked, propping himself up to look at me anxiously while we were still connected. I could feel him growing hard again already.

“Jeez, Caleb. Do you really have to ask?”

He grinned. “Sometimes it’s nice just to hear you say it. Now what do you say we take this into the bedroom?”

“Only if you make me feel like that again,” I smiled back.

“I think I can manage that,” he promised, as he lifted me up, his powerful arms holding me close while he carried me through to his room in the cabin. Carefully, he laid me down on the bed, brushing my hair away from my face as he kissed me tenderly.

“You’re mine, Shelby,” he told me. “Now and forever. Nothing’s going to keep us apart ever again.”

And then he made me see fireworks again. Three times.

Chapter Seven

I woke up with a smile on my face after a night free from nightmares. I reached out for Caleb, hoping that we could take up where we'd left off last night, but as I patted the bed, it became clear that I was alone.

"Caleb?" I called, throwing off the sheets and heading towards the lounge without bothering to cover up. After all, we were on our own in a cabin in the middle of the woods, so there wasn't any risk of frightening the neighbors. Besides, I'd left my clothes where they'd landed after we went to bed, so I had nothing to wear anyway.

"Caleb?" I could see someone sitting in one of the chairs in the lounge, but as they turned to face me, I realized that it wasn't him. I screamed, d wrapping my arms around my body in a vain attempt to protect my modesty before darting back into the bedroom, slamming the door behind me and hoping that whoever it was hadn't just seen me naked.

I desperately looked around the room, trying to find something to put on. Desperately, I opened up drawers until I found some of Caleb's things. I threw on a shirt, but his pants were far too big and I couldn't see any belts to keep them up.

I heard the door open behind me and I whirled round, bending over to stretch the shirt to cover as much of myself as possible in case it was the stranger.

"Shelby? Are you all right? I heard a scream." I turned to see Caleb standing in the doorway, a tray in his hand.

"Caleb!" I gasped, relief flooding through me. "Where were you? I thought you'd abandoned me."

"You really think I would have walked out on you after last night?" He frowned as he crossed over to put the tray on the bedside table. "I know I've got a lot of work to do to earn your trust, but I would have thought you'd know that I'd never leave you like this. No, I went to arrange for someone to open up Tulips."

“Tulips!” I slapped myself on the forehead. I couldn’t believe that I’d managed to forget about my business so easily. “I am such a dumbass. How could you let me sleep in like that?”

“I figured you could do with the rest,” Caleb shrugged. “After all, I kept you up late last night and I know that you’ve been working way too hard recently. You deserve some time off. I’d made a note of Jess’ number when I helped you out in the store and I gave her a call to make sure she could open up this morning. I also called in a favor and got someone to go in and help her out. You can relax. Your store is in safe hands.”

“Even so,” I said firmly. “I should really get going. I’m sure whoever you’ve found is great, but it’s still my store and I need to make sure that everything’s okay.”

“Well you’re not going anywhere until you’ve had some food at least,” Caleb told me, putting his hands on my shoulders and guiding me back to bed. “I was hoping that you’d still be sleeping so I could wake you with breakfast, but I guess there are certain advantages to you being up."

He bent down and kissed me, lightly flicking out his tongue to run across my lips. My fists clenched around a handful of his shirt as he pushed me back onto the bed.

"No. Wait." It took all my willpower to tell him to stop, but I drew away. "I can't do this."

"Why? What's wrong?" Caleb frowned.

"Well in case you'd forgotten, it's not exactly easy for me to keep it quiet and I don't know about you, but I can't enjoy myself when I know there's someone in the next room, listening."

"Ah." Caleb looked sheepish. "I'd forgotten about Josh."

As if he could hear us talking about him, there was a knock at the door.

"I'm guessing these belong to you." Josh opened the door just enough to put his arm through, holding out my clothes as he made a big show of trying not to look at me. “Sorry if I frightened you earlier. I didn’t realize Caleb had company.”

“Thanks, Josh.” Caleb crossed over and took the clothes from him. He said something I couldn’t hear before firmly shutting the door and coming back to sit next to me on the bed. “Now where were we?”

He started kissing my neck, but I pushed him away again.

“Sorry, Caleb. I just can’t do it right now. It doesn’t seem right.”

“It’s okay. Josh has gone out. He’s promised me that we’ll have the place to ourselves for the next few hours.”

“And I really appreciate that. But I’ve got a business I need to go back to and much as I’d love to do nothing but fool around, this is all moving way too fast for me. I need some time to adjust to having you back in my life, think about everything you’ve told me. It’s a lot to take in.”

Caleb looked away, jaw clenched. “All right,” was all he said at last. “I understand. But could you at least have some food with me before I take you back?"

"Sure. That would be lovely."

Caleb tucked me back in bed and placed the tray on my lap. My heart melted when I saw what he'd done. There were fresh scrambled eggs and bacon, as well as a stack of pancakes and a glass of freshly squeezed orange juice.

"Wow. You want to be careful, Caleb," I warned him taking a bite of the lightest, fluffiest eggs I'd ever tasted. "You're setting the bar really high. Keep this up and I'll be expecting breakfast in bed every day."

"I don't mind," he shrugged. "I figure I've got years of spoiling you to make up for. This is just the start."

If Caleb wanted to treat me like this every day, I wasn't going to complain. This was the best breakfast I'd had in a long time.

"So who's Josh?" I asked, tucking into the pancakes.

"He's my cousin," Caleb explained. "And he's very apologetic for frightening you like that. He wasn't supposed to be here today. He'd forgotten that I'd arranged to have the cabin to myself for the week."

"The week?" My eyes boggled. "Did you really think that I'd take a week off work just like that?"

Caleb shrugged modestly. "Maybe, maybe not. Either way, I thought that it wouldn't hurt to have somewhere to retreat to, somewhere away from everything else you've got going on. I figured we would have a lot of talking to do and it would be easiest to do that away from any distractions."

"Talking. That's what you call last night. Uh-huh." I took another bite of pancakes as I nodded sarcastically.

"I mean it, Shelby." He reached forward to tuck my hair behind my ear. "We've got so much time to make up for. I don't want to waste another second. I was hoping that I could persuade you to take some vacation. I'm sure that Jess could look after things for a few days and it's not exactly far to go back in the event of a flower based emergency."

"Jess?" I snorted with laughter. "Don't get me wrong. She's a great assistant, but she's nowhere near ready to run the place. I wouldn't put it past her to shut up shop early if her mom needed a babysitter and anyway, did you forget about the help wanted sign? I need to be taking on more staff right now, not abandoning the place."

"I didn't forget," Caleb said smugly. "I told you. I called in a few favors. I think you'll find that Tulips is in very good hands."

"Well if you don't mind, I like to see for myself," I replied, finishing off the last of the food and pushing away the tray so that I could get dressed.

"My shirt suits you," remarked Caleb, lying across the bed to enjoy the view as I leaned over to pick up my things.

I turned and did a little dance, playing with the bottom of the shirt to hint at a strip tease.

"Now that's just not fair," groaned Caleb. "If you're not careful, I'm going to drag you back to bed."

I laughed and shrugged. "Later."

At last, I was dressed and ready to go. Caleb came and took me in his arms.

"Promise me one thing," he asked.

"What?"

"That when you see that the store is doing fine without you, you'll come and spend the rest of the week with me here."

"And what if it's not doing fine?" I folded my arms and glared at him, not convinced that he was taking my concerns seriously. "Anything could happen. What if there was a sudden big order from one of my corporate clients? Or there was a last minute cancelation and someone needed me to do their wedding?"

"Then I'll come round and personally make sure you have the best week you've ever had. Your sales will sky rocket."

After what he'd achieved in just one day, I didn't doubt that he could deliver.

"All right," I said eventually. "If the store's doing okay and I'm happy that you've found someone I can trust to run the place, I'll come back and spend the week with you."

The smile that spread across Caleb's face could have lit up the room.

"What are we waiting for, then? The sooner we go, the sooner we're back – and the sooner I can get those clothes off again!"

Chapter Eight

My jaw dropped when I walked into the store. Jess was standing behind the counter, wrapping up a bouquet for a customer, while no less than three drop dead gorgeous men were busy helping out around the place.

"Caleb? What's going on?" I turned to him in surprise. "Who are these people?"

"I told you. I called in a few favors," he shrugged, unable to keep the smug look off his face. "Nick over there runs his own floral business in San Diego. He happened to be in the area, so he agreed to come over and look after the place for you along with a couple of his guys. Tulips is in safe hands with him behind the counter."

As Jess said goodbye to her customer, she caught sight of me standing by the door and waved at me.

"Where did you find these people?" she asked wide-eyed as I crossed over to talk to her. "Nick's amazing! I was so worried when you weren't here this morning, but he told me you were taking some vacation." She glanced at Caleb standing next to me, clearly wanting to know what was going on. "I didn't realize you were going away with someone."

I blushed. "Yeah, well it was all very last minute."

Jess looked like she wanted to say something else, but luckily for me, a customer chose that minute to walk in. One of Nick's assistants went over to help, but the moment for gossip had passed, as Nick came forward to introduce himself.

"Hi. You must be Shelby. You're every bit as beautiful as Caleb told me you were." He held out a hand for me to shake. As I touched his hand, I felt a jolt of power running through me. I had a sudden vision in my head of a Kodiak bear.

"You're a shifter too?" The question came out before I could stop it, but Nick didn't seem to take offence.

"I am," he nodded.

Damn. I don't know what it was, but there was definitely something about shifter men that made them sexy. Nick was slightly taller than Caleb with jet black hair and piercing blue eyes. If she wasn't careful, there was no way that Jess would be able to get any work done with him about the place. She'd been distracted enough by Caleb and she'd only spent five minutes with him. One week with Nick and she'd be a wreck!

"I hope you don't mind," Nick went on, "but I thought I might rearrange the displays a little. There's a few little tricks that have worked really well in my store that I think you'll like."

"Go ahead," I told him, although I had a feeling that the reason why his business did well had a lot more to do with how he looked rather than the way the flowers were laid out. "But are you sure you don't mind spending a week here?"

He smiled and looked over at Caleb. "Caleb has helped me out on more than on occasion. It's about time I returned the favor. And now that I've met you, I can see why he's so keen on whisking you away from here."

"Watch it! She's mine," growled Caleb, but there was no real bite to his words, as he pulled me to one side. "Are you satisfied?"

"You haven't done too badly," I conceded. "Nick certainly seems to know what he's doing. I'd still like to spend a bit of time here, though, make sure that he knows how everything works. I also need to get back to my apartment, pack a few things for the week and make sure everything's all right at home."

"All right." Caleb checked his watch. "I've got a few things I need to get done in town. Why don't I pick you up from your place at noon?"

"Why can't I meet you back at the cabin?"

"It's a funny thing. Part of the magic of the place is that only members of the clan can find the entrance."

"So that's why I never noticed that turn off before?"

"Uh-huh," Caleb nodded. "It's also why I couldn't let you follow me there in your car. There was a possibility that I'd take the turn off and you'd lose me. There's a lot of magic in that place. I didn't think you'd believe me unless you saw for yourself."

He was right there. It was becoming increasingly clear that there was a lot going on that I didn't understand. How many more secrets were there for me to uncover?

"Okay," I agreed. "I'll meet you back at my place at midday. That should give me enough time to get everything done. The address is-"

"It's all right," Caleb interrupted me. "You don't need to tell me. That's part of the magic of you being my mate. No matter how far away you are, I'll always be able to find you."

He lightly kissed me and turned to leave as I watched him go. I couldn't stop the stupid grin spreading across my face as

I brought my hand up to feel where his lips had been a moment ago.

Just as he walked past the window, he turned into a bear, rearing up outside the store to wave at me.

“What about your shirt?” I laughed, shaking my head as he shambled off into the city. I should have known that when he stripped off last night, it was just to show off his abs.

“He’s a shifter?” gasped Jess. “And your boyfriend? Wow. I’ve heard that shifter sex is *hot*. Is it true that they can control every part of their body?”

I shot her a dark look. “Did you forget that you’re talking to your boss?” I reminded her pointedly.

“Sorry.” Jess bit her lip and looked down.

“Right. Now I need to talk to Nick about what’s happening this week, since I’ll be away for a few days, so you’re in charge out here while we talk out back. Nick? Could you come with me, please?”

The shifter followed me through to the staff area at the back of the store, where I pulled out the order book to talk him through everything we had on that week.

"I've got a couple of big weddings coming up," I told him, "so you might find that you get calls from the brides to confirm a few details. Just make a note in this book of any changes and if any of them feel that they absolutely definitely have to talk to me, you can give them my cell, which is written up on the contact list on the board over there."

"Give them your cell," echoed Nick. "Got it."

As I flipped through the book, I was glad that Caleb had chosen this week to whisk me away. There was no way that I could have agreed to take a vacation if I had a wedding booked. Nick might be amazing at what he did, but this was still my business and I'd spent too long building up good relationships with all my clients to be happy letting someone else cover such an important event for me.

"There are a couple of regular corporate clients that might call," I went on. "The details of their usual orders are in this book *here.*" I pulled out another ledger and talked Nick through what my clients expected and when. It was clear from the kinds of questions he asked that he knew his stuff and the more we talked, the more relaxed I felt about leaving the store under his supervision for a few days.

It felt so good to be able to talk to someone who understood my industry. Most people's eyes started to glaze over when you began to compare notes on your favorite combinations of flowers and color matching. Nick was as enthusiastic about flowers as I was, his face lighting up when he talked about the time he'd provided flowers for a movie set.

I was so lost in his stories that I forgot to keep an eye on the time. There was just so much to talk about!

"Didn't Caleb say that he was going to pick you up at noon?" asked Nick suddenly, nudging me and pointing to the clock hanging on the wall.

"Oh no!" I wailed when I realized that I had barely enough time to get home before Caleb was due to come and get me, let alone pack anything.

"Don't worry. If I know Caleb, he won't mind waiting for you a little longer for you, not after all these years. You know, in all the time I've known him, there's only ever been one woman for him and now that I've met you, I can understand why. Caleb's a lucky guy."

I didn't know what to say to that, so I smiled nervously as I gathered my things together and went out to check on Jess.

"Now you're sure you're going to be all right with Nick and-" I realized that I hadn't actually asked for the names of his assistants.

"Matt and Justin," Jess filled in for me. "Yes, I'm going to be totally fine."

Fine wasn't the half of it. Something told me that Jess was going to go out of her way to spend as much time at work as possible with the three men. They were certainly easy on the eye and I was already beginning to wonder whether I'd be able to persuade Nick to let Matt or Justin stay on after I came back to work. It would certainly save me trying to find someone of their caliber.

"Are you sure?" I double checked. "I mean, I'm just on the end of a cell if you need me for anything."

"Positive," Jess urged, pushing me towards the door. "Now it's my turn to tell you to leave. If I had someone like Caleb coming to pick me up, I wouldn't be doing my best to be late. If there's any problems, I'll call, but I can guarantee that there won't be."

"Okay, okay, I'm going," I laughed, casting one last look about the place before walking out.

Luckily, my apartment wasn't far from the store and I was able to change quickly before starting throwing a few things in a case before I heard Caleb knocking on the door.

"I'm sorry," I said as I opened the door, but I was stopped from saying anything else as Caleb stepped forward, swept me up in his arms and kissed me hard.

"You were saying?" he grinned when we finally broke apart.

"Oh… err…" I could barely think straight. Caleb had such a devastating effect on me that made it impossible to concentrate.

"Unless you're attempting to cancel, you've got nothing to apologize for," he told me, as he walked into my apartment.

"No, no. I'm not canceling," I rushed to reassure him. "But I've only just got back home myself, so I haven't had a chance to pack anything."

"That's all right. You won't need any clothes anyway." A flush of heat rushed through me as Caleb pulled me towards him. I could feel his erection pressing against me and I closed my eyes as I tried to quell the wave of lust.

"I do need *some* things," I pointed out. "What if Josh decides to hang around?"

"He won't." Caleb's eyes darkened. "And I'm sorry that he startled you. I've made sure that he won't come anywhere near the cabin. We've got the place completely to ourselves for the next few days. I promise."

"Well in that case, give me five minutes and I'll be right with you."

I rushed into my room and began to throw things into my bag. I had no intention of spending the entire week naked, even if Caleb was the sexiest guy on the planet – and he was definitely a strong contender for the title.

At last, I had everything I needed and I went out to meet Caleb, expecting to find him sitting on my sofa, but he wasn't there.

"Caleb?"

My apartment wasn't exactly large and there were a limited number of places where he could be hiding. I went into the kitchen to see if he was fixing himself a drink, but there was no sign of him.

“Caleb?” My cries became more frantic, but there was no reply.

“Caleb!” I sank to the floor, choking back a sob as I returned to that young girl who’d lost her love. Once again, he’d walked out on me with no explanation and no clue to where he’d gone.

Chapter Nine

I couldn't believe what had happened. Caleb couldn't have been playing me, could he? He'd never been cruel though and his explanation for why he'd walked out had made perfect sense – unless he was lying to me.

I pulled myself together, refusing to shed one more tear over him. I wasn't a schoolgirl anymore. I was a grown woman. If Caleb thought he could disappear on me again, then he was in for a rude awakening. I was going to find him and give him a piece of my mind.

"Think, Shelby, think," I muttered to myself, pulling myself up to pace the floor. None of this made any sense. Why would Caleb have gone to all the trouble of arranging temporary staff at my store if he was suddenly going to skip town?

I looked around for a note, but there was nothing. I checked my cell, but he hadn't bothered to call or text me either.

Something felt horribly wrong. Maybe Caleb was in trouble and needed my help? There had to be a way of finding him. There had to be.

I closed my eyes and thought about him, seeing his face in my mind. I pictured his smile, remembered the feel of his skin against mine, the scent of his aftershave.

Suddenly I had a vision of a familiar place. My eyes flew open. I knew where he was!

I snatched up my car keys and raced down to my car. The second the ignition fired, I screeched out of the spot, not caring about the blaring horn from the vehicle I narrowly missed driving into.

I headed north, up towards the Bridge. Maybe some might say that I was just using logic, that the most obvious place to look for him was at his family's land, but there was more to it than that. Some instinct told me that he was back at the clan base, an instinct that I could physically feel in the pit of my stomach. Caleb was unhurt for now, but I could tell that he was nervous about something and I didn't like the thought that he might be in danger.

As I got further and further away from the city, I put my foot down, not caring about the speed limit. Caleb needed me and nothing was going to keep us apart, not this time.

Drawing closer to the turn off, the feeling in my belly grew stronger until it was almost painful.

"Hold on, Caleb. I'm coming!" I called as I saw the narrow trail I needed to go down. Spinning the steering wheel to the right, I didn't care if I scratched the sides of my car, my usual caution forgotten in my desperation to help my lover. If another car was coming in the opposite direction, neither of us would stand a chance, but that was a risk I was willing to take if it meant that I could save Caleb.

At last, I hit the car park. Just as I had seen, Caleb's car was right there and I pulled up alongside it. However, he wasn't alone. There were two other cars next to his and as I locked up, I wondered what was going on when Caleb had promised me we were going to have the place to ourselves all week.

"Aargh!"

A terrifying scream split the air and I doubled over in pain as the sensation in my stomach intensified.

Was someone torturing Caleb?

I looked around for something to use as a weapon, but all I could find was a large stick. Still, if I was able to creep up on someone, I might be able to knock them out with it, so I picked it up and headed off in the direction of the scream.

As I moved closer to the sound, my whole body seemed to be drawn towards it. It was as though there was something inside me, pulling me closer to Caleb. I didn't care if I fought them with my bare hands. No one was going to hurt my man!

"Aargh!"

The scream had changed, the sound seeming to be mixed with the roar of a bear. My head was filled with visions of someone forcing Caleb to shift against his will and my heart almost broke at the sound. I couldn't imagine how much agony would be behind a cry like that.

"Aargh!"

"I'm here, Caleb!" I yelled, rushing out into the middle of a clearing, brandishing my cudgel high over my head to fight off whoever was hurting him, but when I saw what was waiting for me, I froze, the stick falling from my hands.

Chapter Ten

"Stay right where you are, Shelby" ordered Caleb carefully. Standing in front of me was the strangest thing I'd ever seen. A young man who was barely in his twenties was halfway between human and bear shape, his body all bent and misshapen in some strange combination of the two. As he screamed again, his arm stretched further than I would ever have imagined possible, filling out to become more bearlike.

I didn't need to be told twice. I had no intention of moving.

"It's all right, Tyler," Caleb soothed, slowly moving round to try and get between me and the new shifter. "You're safe. It's all right. No one is going to hurt you here."

"Leave. Me. ALONE!" Tyler lashed out with his paw, backhanding Caleb, sending him flying. He crashed into a tree trunk and slid to the floor, stunned.

I squeezed my eyes tightly as Tyler lunged at me, holding my breath as I braced myself for an attack that never came. When I realized that nothing had happened, I opened first one, and then the other, looking down to see Tyler on all fours in front of me, his change taking over and forcing him to the ground. Although it was impossible to see exactly what was changing, he was becoming more and more bear with every passing moment.

Although my mind was screaming at me to run away, a little voice inside me told me that I was safe, that Tyler didn't want to hurt anyone. He was just in pain and struggling to cope. Trying to control the shaking of my hand, I reached out and stroked Tyler's hair.

"It's all right," I told him. "Everything's going to be all right. Just let it happen."

Tyler whimpered as his body filled out, every change bringing with it excruciating pain.

I carried on stroking his hair as it turned to fur.

"There you go," I whispered. "Almost there."

I knelt down in front of him, taking his face in both hands so that he could look at me.

"It's okay, Tyler," I smiled, willing his pain to go away. "We're here for you. I promise that it gets easier."

At last, his change was complete and Tyler collapsed from exhaustion, lying unconscious on the ground before me.

The second he was gone, I got up and ran over to Caleb, still motionless against the tree. I tore a strip off my shirt and used it to mop away a trickle of blood running down the side of his face.

"Come back to me, Caleb," I whispered, gently kissing his forehead. I put my hand where my lips had been and I felt it warming up. A heat spread from my palm, Caleb's skin soaking it up.

"Sh-shelby?" he moaned, his eyes fluttering open.

"Yes, baby. I'm here." I didn't know whether I was laughing or crying as I helped him stand up. He swayed for a moment before looking around, spotting Tyler on the floor.

"Tyler!" he gasped, rushing over to his side.

"It's all right," I said. "I didn't do anything to him. He finished shifting and then he collapsed."

"The first shift is exhausting," nodded Caleb. "But I don't understand. How are you all right? New shifters lash out all over the place. He was right next to you. I thought he was going to kill you."

"I don't know," I shrugged. "I just spoke to him, told him that he was safe as he transformed. He didn't even try to hurt me."

Caleb checked over the unconscious bear. When he was satisfied that Tyler was okay, he came back to stand in front of me. "There's something else I don't get. How did you manage to find me here?"

"What do you mean?"

"I told you. There's a magic protecting this place. Only clan members can find it. You're not clan."

"Yes, she is."

The pair of us whirled round at the unexpected voice. A man with silver hair who looked more than a little like Caleb was walking towards us.

"Uncle Robert!" Caleb looked stunned. "I didn't think you were back in the country yet."

"Some instinct told me that I needed to be here." He turned to me. "You must be Shelby," he smiled warmly. "Caleb's told us a lot about you and I have to say that you're even more beautiful than he described."

"Th-thanks," I stammered as he took my hand, surprising me by dropping a light kiss on the back of my knuckles.

"How's Tyler doing?" Robert turned to Caleb.

"Okay," he replied, "but it was touch and go for a while. If it wasn't for Shelby, Tyler might not be resting now. For a moment, I thought he was going to go on the rampage, but somehow, Shelby managed to calm him down."

"Did she now?" Robert turned and examined me critically, not bothering to hide it. "Then you are even more special than Caleb told us. Come. Let's go back to the cabin. There's a lot to talk about."

"What about Tyler?" I glanced over at the bear, who let out a tiny snort, apparently dreaming.

"He'll be fine," Robert assured me. "Josh can take care of him."

"Josh?" I glared at Caleb. "I thought you told me he'd left?"

"To be fair, I said that he'd stay away from the cabin," Caleb corrected.

"Look, let's get inside." Robert interrupted us. "I think it's going to rain soon and I don't know about you, but I could do with a drink."

Chapter Eleven

Caleb and I were sitting curled up next to each other on the same sofa where we'd made love while Robert poured us all a glass of wine. Just as he'd predicted, the skies had opened just after we'd arrived at the cabin and the sound of rain drumming on the roof was the background to our discussion.

"How much do you know about shifter lore?" Robert asked, passing me my drink.

"Not a lot," I confessed. "I know that shifters are strong and can heal injuries quickly. I know that the full moon thing is a myth, because shifters can change at any time, but that it's true that silver bullets are the only way to kill a shifter. That's about it."

"So you don't know anything about shifter clans?"

"From what Caleb said, I assume it's the members of a family who are shifters."

"Close, but not quite." Robert tapped the side of his glass with one finger as he thought about how best to explain. "A clan is more than family. Loyalty to your clan comes above all else and sometimes, on rare occasions, a member of a shifting family finds themselves being drawn to a different clan. When that happens, the shifter puts the clan before blood, protecting their clan members no matter what. It's been a long time since the last shifter war, but they're bloody and brutal – and clan comes first. Until you feel the ties of the clan, it's impossible to describe just how deep they run."

"But you still have to be born into it, right?" I asked.

"Not necessarily." It was Caleb's turn to talk and he took my hand as he turned to face me. "You see, shifters mate for life. Nobody really knows how the magic of mating works, just that we're drawn to the person we're meant to be with and nothing will keep us apart after we've found each other."

"Mating brings new blood into the clan," Robert explained. "And every now and then, it also brings along someone extra special, someone like you."

"Me?" I shook my head in disbelief. "I'm nothing special."

"Have you seen yourself in the mirror?" laughed Caleb. "You're beautiful and if you don't believe that, then I'm going to spend the rest of my life showing you how beautiful you really are."

I blushed as Robert picked up the conversation.

"It's more than that," he went on. "Few people could do what you did today with Tyler. When a shifter first changes, we bring them here for everyone's safety. A new shifter is unpredictable and needs the support of our strongest males to make sure they don't hurt themselves or anyone else. Yet you were able to stand in front of him and ease his change."

"That didn't look very easy to me."

"Believe me, Shelby," Caleb said. "Compared to what I went through, Tyler had it easy."

I looked at him and my heart ached to think that I hadn't be able to be there for him.

"Someone like is one in a million. A billion, even," Robert told me. "If you mate with Caleb-"

"Wait a minute." I held up a hand to interrupt. "What do you mean, if?"

"You don't have to mate with Caleb," Robert explained.

"But you told me that we were destined to be together forever?" I turned to Caleb who blushed.

"We are – if you agree to be my mate," he clarified.

"Caleb's right," Robert continued. "You have a choice, unlike the shifters. You can choose to be part of our clan or you can walk out the door right now with no hard feelings. No one will think any worse of you for not wanting to join a shifter clan. There's still a lot of prejudice in this world and it's not an easy path. But if you do decide to join, you'll find there's no better people to be surrounded by than your clan."

I sat there, stunned. It was a lot to take in. "What did you mean when you said that I was one in a million?" I asked.

"Ah yes." Robert smiled. "What you did with Tyler today was magic – literally. The fact that you were able to calm and soothe his bear is a very rare ability."

"As is being able to find your way to me," Caleb put in. "Normally, that only happens after mating. You should never have been able to find the turn off."

"Nothing was going to keep me away from you," I shrugged. "Not even magic."

"So what do you say?" asked Caleb. "Will you be my mate?"

I laughed. "Caleb, I've been your mate since we were in high school. I've always thought we were meant to be together forever. This just confirms it."

Caleb leaned forward to kiss me.

"I'll leave you two alone." I barely heard Robert as he put his glass down and left the cabin.

"I love you, Shelby," Caleb whispered, pressing his forehead against mine, barely able to stop kissing me.

"I love you, too."

Caleb stood and reached out a hand. "Come on. Let's go to bed. It's much more comfortable there than here."

"I don't know." I bit my lip. "I was kind of hoping that we could work our way round all the sofas in here..."

Caleb growled and pounced on me. As he began to caress his way down my body, I knew that we'd never be apart again.

A letter from the author

Hi there. I'm Amber Belmont and I'd like to personally thank you for reading my book. I hope you enjoyed the story as much as I enjoyed writing it. Let me know what you thought by leaving a review – I'd really appreciate it!
I'll be releasing another instalment in the 'Love Laid Bear' series in the next month, so to and get details of all my new releases, ***join my book club*** *at*
writing.amberbelmont.com

Love, Amber

64091654R00070

Made in the USA
Lexington, KY
27 May 2017